W9-ACH-901

DISCARD

Sabrina Sue
Loves the Snow

written and illustrated by
Priscilla Burris

Ready-to-Read

Simon Spotlight

New York   London   Toronto   Sydney   New Delhi

For my beloved East Los Angeles Library

SIMON SPOTLIGHT

An imprint of Simon & Schuster Children's Publishing Division

1230 Avenue of the Americas, New York, New York 10020

This Simon Spotlight edition August 2021

Copyright © 2021 by Priscilla Burris

SIMON SPOTLIGHT, READY-TO-READ, and colophon are registered
trademarks of Simon & Schuster, Inc.

For information about special discounts for bulk purchases, please contact
Simon & Schuster Special Sales at 1-866-506-1949
or business@simonandschuster.com.

Manufactured in the United States of America 0721 LAK

2 4 6 8 10 9 7 5 3 1

Library of Congress Cataloging-in-Publication Data

Names: Burris, Priscilla, author, illustrator.

Title: Sabrina Sue loves the snow / written and illustrated by Priscilla Burris.

Description: Simon Spotlight edition. | New York : Simon Spotlight, 2021. |
Series: Ready-to-read. Level 1 | Summary: Sabrina Sue is a small chicken who lives
on a farm but dreams of faraway places, and one day she decides to go and see the
snow, so she finds a place that has snow and sets out by truck and train to get there.

Identifiers: LCCN 2021005252 (print) | LCCN 2021005253 (ebook) | ISBN
9781534484474 (hardcover) | ISBN 9781534484467 (paperback) |
ISBN 9781534484481 (ebook)

Subjects: LCSH: Chickens—Juvenile fiction. | Voyages and travels—Juvenile fiction.
| Snow—Juvenile fiction. | Farms—Juvenile fiction. | CYAC: Chickens—Fiction. |
Voyages and travels—Fiction. | Snow—Fiction. | Farm life—Fiction.

Classification: LCC PZ7.B5229 Sb 2021 (print) | LCC PZ7.B5229 (ebook) | DDC [E]—dc23

LC record available at https://lccn.loc.gov/2021005252

LC ebook record available at https://lccn.loc.gov/2021005253

Sabrina Sue lived on a farm.

On a very hot day, she thought about snow.

She always wanted to see
snow.

She asked about snow.

She daydreamed about it.

Her farm friends knew she wanted to see snow.

Sabrina Sue liked being goofy and silly sometimes. Should she stay on the farm?

I really do want to feel cold snow.
She thought and thought.

She found a place where it snowed a lot and made a plan.

She packed snow clothes.

Farmer Martha's truck was the first ride.

Next she got on a train.

The train rumbled.

She jumbled this way and
that way.

She looked out the window.
She saw mountains with
snow on top of them!
She was getting close.

Sabrina Sue put on her snow clothes.

It was time to get off the
train.

She walked over a bridge.

She hiked under big rocks.

Then she saw it.

Snow!

Snow is fun!

Sabrina Sue loved the
snow.

She thought about her
farm friends.

It was time to go home.

Sabrina Sue was happy to be back on the farm.

But one day she would visit the snow again!